Beatrice & Phillip

BY

Jim McGuiggan

© *Jim McGuiggan - 2018*

All rights reserved

This little book is for a few of many truly wonderful women I have met down the years and have come to know and greatly admire; Women in whom beauty and strength in their finest forms made a home:

Peggy Blanton
Ali Campbell
Dorothy Cheney
Virginia Chitwood
Carol Crisp
Kathy Davis
Marge Hoover
Kay Jackson
Mariana Long
Cassie McGuiggan
Velinda McWherter
Jeanne Moore
Karen Nance
Billie Paine
Jeannine Patrick
Beth Weaver
Beverly Wright

INTRODUCTION

You will recognize quickly that this little book is an old and often told story revisited. But there are enough departures from the customary telling of that story for me to say it isn't the "same old story." My hope is that you might you would find it enjoyable reading and that maybe here and there there's something worth reflecting on.

Jmcg

2017

Beatrice & Phillip

A Short Story on Life and Love

Contents

BREAKFAST AT THE PEARSON HOUSE 11

BAD TIDINGS & THE BEGINNING OF TOIL 17

THE GRAND AFFAIR 23

BEHOLD THE COMING OF THE BEAST 33

THE MANSION OF DESPAIR & HOPE, LIFE, & DEATH 39

THE STORM 47

THE MEETING 51

THE LEAVING, THE OFFENSE & THE AGREEMENT ... 57

THE RETURN, THE STORY & THE DEPARTURE 69

BEATRICE & THE BEAST 73

THROUGH A DOOR DARKLY 77

FACE TO FACE 87

A SURPRISE MEETING AND A MYSTERY SOLVED 97

DREAMS AND QUESTIONS 103

JOY & PAIN: THE GRAND AFFAIR REVISITED 111

LOVE SHARED & LOVE UNREQUITED 121

SETTING BEATRICE FREE 129

THE RETURN TO HOME 135

HOME, THE JOY & THE LONGING 137

BACK TO A BELOVED FRIEND 139

THE MIRACULOUS POWER OF LOVE 149

CHAPTER 1

BREAKFAST AT THE PEARSON HOUSE

Freshly baked bread, eggs, bacon, fruit, cheese, cereal—not a common breakfast in the region but common enough to the six Pearsons who enjoyed the entire experience; the food *and* the company, I mean.

The house was large and very comfortable. Every room had at least one painting by the mother, Jacqueline, an accomplished amateur artist that was fully content to *be* an amateur and a baker of bread in the early morning that would make a cuckoo-clock hungry. The father, Henry Ellison Pearson, was an experienced, hard-working and careful investor in trade and commodities. The son Robert, the oldest child, was a senior bank clerk—he worked in the foreign currency department and there were two very attractive daughters (Georgina and

Jennifer)—all at the table when the third and youngest girl made her entrance. She didn't walk in. As was her custom she glided in, swaying and gesturing as all great teenage ballerinas did. Beatrice, not as pretty as the older sisters, stretched and gestured as she hummed the dance music from some ballet or other that suited her mood and movements. The usual protests went up from the sisters as she hovered around them, dragging flimsy lace netting over their heads and faces while egg or buttered bread was on its way to their mouths. "Father, will you tell her to stop…" spluttered Jennifer. Robert advised them to ignore her rather than encourage her with protests. That was a mistake that earned the young banker the ballerina's full attention. The parents were non-responsive other than rolling their eyes at each other and smiling wryly. Who really wanted to change her? The dancer then became an actress recently out of the silent movie era, mouthing melodramatic Garbo-type sentences offered from behind a lace table cover. Then came the acknowledging of the applause that wasn't offered, the kind rejection of the calls for "encore" that never sounded and kisses all around the table that the siblings endured for fear of provoking more. And there was a long, gentle hug for the father while he slipped his arm around her and kissed her. Clearly, she was the favorite of the household; a good singer, one who played very well a number of instruments and a keen gardener that specialized in flowers. As the years slipped by Beatrice would change but not a lot; she'd still be musical, dramatic and happiest when she was in her garden with the flowers. Her favorite flowers were roses but for a reason she couldn't uncover they didn't do well nor had she seen them do well in any garden in the district. She spoke about it to her father who traveled quite a bit and he promised he'd find the answer somewhere.

This was a well -to-do family though not enormously rich. The breakfast table was well spread but not lavishly. A swift glance at their clothing, furniture, the numerous rooms and furnishings all indicated that they enjoyed a comfortable living. They loved and liked each other.

On the morning I have particularly in mind, as the lively conversations continued Robert leaned over and quietly asked his father about a recent major business transaction. His tone said there was reason for concern. "The other thing going ahead all right?" It had something to do with a very large loan Henry had secured for a European industrial corporation—a loan he would need to repay if the corporation that currently was suffering major setbacks collapsed. "It's too soon to tell. I've seen recovery from worse situations," the father said for Robert's ears only. "But I'd sleep better at night if things were different," he sighed and then calmly rose from the table.

CHAPTER 2

BAD TIDINGS & THE BEGINNING OF TOIL

Everyone went about their business and weeks became months. Henry stayed busy at other ventures but was often on the phone about the matter of chief concern. The outcome was still in the balance. Pearson fully understood this and took it patiently but he was also a shrewd business man and when a letter arrived from Europe he opened it with dread. From a good friend and Board member:

"My dear Pearson; terrible news...Formal communication to follow...

Profoundest regret, Dumont."

The lengthy struggle began and with the years it became more intense. From comfortably well-off to eventual heavy borrowing to stay afloat; borrowing that made it even harder to stay afloat and requests for loans denied. That was the story though Henry assured the family that things would work out. There could be no quick fix, he reminded them repeatedly, and it would mean he would be gone from home a lot but no one was to lose heart. This they were sure of, he continued to tell them, "Come what may we still have one another—money matters but we have what matters most."

The children worked, fell in love, married and got on with living while the parents and Beatrice moved a third time to accommodations in keeping with their new economic state. A long term heart-condition took the adored Jacqueline, the family was devastated and Henry lost much of his energy for business and if there was any sense of adventure left in battling the odds—that began to hemorrhage away as well. Must-do can be a good master sometimes and there were substantial loan payments to be met so the honorable man worked without slacking to make contacts and generate new investors in worthy and sound projects. He and Beatrice, though always very close, were now closer. The married children were getting by financially but it was simply beyond them to significantly help the father though they fervently wished they could — life went on.

"Aren't you ready to get married, Beatrice?" the father asked her as he packed for yet another trip. He had begun to look older than his years and his daughter took note of it.

"Get married and leave you?" she said laughing. "Heavens no! I couldn't be happier if I had tailored my life. I have brothers and sisters I love and who love me and I have a father I adore and who adores me. What more is there? I live a dream come true."

"I wish *that* were true my dear," he sighed, "but a lovely young woman like you needs more than work and being stuck here at home alone much of the time. I hate it! I wish…"

"Papa," Beatrice insisted, "I have music, books, a job I like at the library, this comfortable little house and my beautiful garden. Wait and see, one of these days I'll grow the finest roses ever seen and I'll be famous." She giggled and then she said as she put her arms around him, "And you, Papa; I have *you!* What more could I want? And, you know, I always have the sense that though we're going through difficult times there's someone looking out for us. You believe that too, don't you, Papa! Truly, I need nor want anything more right now. Romance? — I'd rather have what we have together than that. Besides, I'd never find a husband like you."

He held her close, not believing half she said but thanking God for such a daughter, and off he went saying, "This will probably be a lengthy trip so don't be worrying and take care, my love." He looked around as he heard her shout after him, "Papa, bring me a lovely rose for my garden if you find one!"

CHAPTER 3

THE GRAND AFFAIR

A very fancy letter. In her mail-box. That's what she found when she came home from work one afternoon and there, in the street, she opened it and in fact it wasn't a letter; it was an invitation to a grand dinner and musical evening. She looked around immediately, sure that there must have been a mistake but a pleasant and hawk-eyed neighbor across the street assured her that a well-dressed man had checked the address before putting it in the box.

"But who...how...?" she thought. She read it again; all the needed information was there along with the host's name but no guest's name — it was apparently an open invitation. "You Are Invited to..."All was mystery, and a perplexed Beatrice was still sure a mistake must have been made. Still, it *had* been delivered to *her* house by someone who had checked the address.

She'd never been to anything really grand but maybe, and this she wished to believe, maybe her father in earlier days had somehow made contact with this very rich man who owned the mansion well outside of town; maybe that was the explanation. For all her real and lingering doubt that was the explanation she settled for and the idea of a *musical* evening did the rest. Like everyone else in the area she had heard of the great house and the occasional grand affairs that were held there; how could they not have heard? Some thought they knew the name of the wealthy owner but no one had ever been near the house. For all kinds of reasons, good and bad, the very wealthy have little or nothing to do with the working class beneath them and for all kinds of reasons the working class return the sentiment.

The following week, all prettied up she drove her little horse and trap a long way outside of town and drove through the open gate into the grounds. There it was—a huge house with light pouring from countless windows, shining on the many grand carriages sitting everywhere. That was enough and she was in the act of turning her horse, intending to drive back home when the beautiful music streamed out of the house, alluring, inviting. There was no doubt about it, this gathering was beyond her station but...but there *was* the invitation, there was the curiosity, there was the hunger to experience another world and then there was the music—yes, the wonderful music and before she knew it was at the door.

Fear had her heartbeat in her throat but she took a deep breath, smoothed out her simple dress and approached the royally-dressed footman at the door with an air of confidence that was no part of her. He took the card without taking his eyes off her. Visibly uncertain he glanced at the card now in his gloved hand, looked again at the pleasant young woman and then scrutinized the card while she waited. Her appearance said there was a mistake but the invitation card spoke with authority. He couldn't turn her away or leave her standing there while he went in search of a decision from who he didn't know. Heavens, what if the one he was hesitating about was related to one of the honored guests? What if she was a quirky nonconformist friend of the family? He began to stutter something when Beatrice heard herself, say, "Well? Must I stand here all evening, my man?" making as if she was about to push past him. That did it, he dropped his eyes, begged her pardon, welcomed her in and wished her a wonderful evening.

The grand hall, the beautiful chandeliers, the orchestra, the laughter, the conversations, the stunning dresses, the jewelry and numerous dancing couples—she definitely didn't belong here but she was in it now and would attempt to make the best of it. Not many things claimed more attention that an out-of-place wallflower, sad and forlorn and the last thing she wanted was an excess of attention; but that's just what she got. The "beautiful people" discreetly moved away when she came in their direction—away as though they hadn't seen her and then took full stock of her when her back was to them. There were raised eyebrows, smiles and puzzled looks, nods that informed others and some obviously offended guests—they were all there while Beatrice wove her way through the crowd. Awkwardness and awe wrestled with each other in her mind but awe won as she made her way close to the orchestra and stood mesmerized.

The report of a gate-crashing undesirable that lowered the tone of the gathering passed from mouth to mouth and those who hadn't yet seen the intruder scrambled to get a glimpse. The word soon reached the handsome young host who was moving among the large crowd, affecting an air of modesty with a little "it's-nothing-really wave of the hand but greedily seeking, getting and drinking in the syrupy congratulations offered. Immediately embarrassed and enraged by the report he had the head footman brought to him and there, in the presence of his offended guests, he harangued and humiliated the poor man.

"But she had an invitation, sir. You can be sure I checked it carefully when I saw her. Here, see for yourself."

How dare the stammering footman defend himself and give a perfectly good reason for his accepting this person as a guest? How dare this lowly specimen make his superior seem totally unreasonable? How dare he respectfully and quietly continue to further explain his action? The host now even more furious felt compelled to justify his rage and unbridled speech. He would make an example of the fool so with his voice rising and the nearer segments of the great crowd going silent, transfixed by the spectacle, he snarled. "Have you no eyes, man? Could you not see…?" The ranting reached her and though frightened Beatrice could not remain out of sight. Vigorously she pushed aside the protesting grandees in her way she began to speak gently but clearly in the servant's defense to the incensed host who now had the servant by the scruff of his neck, shaking him and assuring him, "I will see to it that you will never work again." Then the words of the girl! The astonished and then horrified look on the tyrant's face couldn't be missed. First, to be educated by a mere servant he was now to be subjected to instruction from a nameless working-class intruder? He released his grip on the footman, leaned over and thundered into the young girl's face. "Be quiet!" That frightened and silenced her immediately and at a nod from him a man stepped forward and dragged the quietly protesting Beatrice away to a room off the kitchen. There she waited and waited and waited to see what was to happen and if she would be given an opportunity to fully explain. Someone noisily set a plate of food down before her while the great crowd was guided into a grand dining hall. The treatment by the whispering and glancing kitchen-workers was cold and without a word to her and finally she ran sobbing from the room, found the right doors, pushed her way through the moving crowd in the grand hall and out into the kindness of the night that would hide her tears but couldn't ease the pounding of her breaking heart or cool the scalding heat of humiliation. The servant soon followed, shoved out the door and sent sprawling into the darkness. The heartless host had a satisfied look on his face.

"Serves him right for not protecting us from low class party-crashers. Serves her right. Invitation or not, she should have known better than to come into a gathering of the finest of people then she wouldn't have had the experience of being compelled to go out." At this, there were vigorous nods and numerous cries of "Hear, hear." He concluded his remarks with a smile and, "Ah well, a little bit of distraction and amusement, something you can tell your friends and children about."

Several days later her father returned with a story of promises made to him, assurances that his listeners would think over his proposals but without tangible success. "Still," he said, "One never knows when these meetings will pay off."

She enthusiastically agreed with him but shared the disappointment that lay beneath the words. "And you, my dear, how have you been while I've been away? She gave him a happy report and said nothing at all about the *grand affair* and her frequent sobbing in the night when the memory of it rose unbidden. Henry Pearson continued his travels and the weeks became months and the months stretched into several years. Weary and often discouraged the good-hearted man remained at his task. He owed honorable debts and like many men and women on integrity he would see them repaid. And he had Beatrice and her future to secure—for her he'd tear down the sky if he could. Those throughout the region who might have seen this often weary man had caught sight of one of humanity's lovelier sights.

CHAPTER 4

BEHOLD THE COMING OF THE BEAST

It was in the middle of his unprecedented business success that Phillip Durand began to experience little but definite changes in his physical well-being; they came and went. There was no loss of energy, no feeling that he was "ill" but there was no mistaking their presence or that they were slowly developing. At first he doubted them because he wanted to but it finally became clear that denial was a mistake for as the months went by they returned more quickly and some of them didn't completely leave. He was a handsome young man and vain—a truth emphasized by the excessive number of mirrors in his house. The time he spent in front of them looking for every little change was not surprising nor were the frequent house-calls by physicians of various kinds. These were the best doctors available and they guessed this and that and suggested this treatment and that.

The numerous medical test reports came in, were read, crumpled and flung into the flames in the great fireplace. "Nothing to worry about, my dear Sir," "Merely an attack of inflammation; will take of itself." "An infection that a will clear up in a month if you take…" "Avoid eating…"

"Quacks," he snarled and sent for others. After examinations and treatments for more than a year by the most acclaimed professors that fame and wealth could secure, treatments that brought no relief or assurance, his alarm knew no bounds and his rage grew with the symptoms. He became utterly heartless in his business dealings for why should he be compassionate when life was heartless toward him? If ever there had been any patience it was now obliterated. Competitors were hounded and their companies devoured and he became the most feared force in the business world; but as the vast wealth poured in Niagara-like his peace of mind streamed out through gaping wounds in his mind. For a while the grand affairs continued in his name but the host was no longer present and finally, putting his financial affairs into the hands of skilled and completely trustworthy financiers he disappeared and grand affairs ceased. While in seclusion the rumors about him spread but the rumors were not as shocking as the reality.

The mysterious disease began to show itself in hypertrichosis but it didn't end there. Over time it affected his eyes that became blood red. Jaw-bones grew, teeth were displaced and turned a dull yellow, gums swelled, his vocal chords lengthened and his voice deepened and sounded guttural. The spine suffered so that he walked slouched forward; the arms, feet and legs were affected with marked swelling and some twisting, his ears beneath the hair were misshapen and though the hands were not just as badly affected as other parts, under the hair his fingers were gnarled and his nails were like claws. Breathing became difficult, often wheezy and always noisy. He completed his seclusion by fleeing to one of his beautiful mansions in a fenced-off section of dense forest area he owned. There he paced the rooms as the horror reached its limit and in the only mirror he tolerated in the huge many-roomed house he finally beheld *a Beast*. He raged and screamed like the strange thing that glared back at him, making sounds and yelling words in that voice that was no longer his own—all that had come to pass and he moved nearer and nearer toward sanity unhinged. Sleepless nights were the usual but exhaustion brought sporadic periods of sleep that perhaps helped and brought him back from the edge of the abyss where he spent so much of his time. In the long period that passed he wrote a rare personal letter left just outside the fence to be delivered by those who knew how to mind their own business and ask no questions whatever. They were rewarded well enough to regularly visit the place and so the rare notes made their way to the very few that still remembered him or cared at all to remember. It was a soul-killing loneliness that led him to write anything at all. It was his awful deformity that demanded he remain utterly alone. For, this he knew, there was no love or friendship in the world that could endure such deformity, such *difference*. Was he not himself repulsed by grossly disfigured people that would have looked beautiful when compared with him? And so once in a very great while he would scrawl:

"I continue to be desperately ill but do not fear dying—I fear not dying. To live long like this, never to be free, is my worst nightmare and so when I sleep, though I rarely do, I dream of horror and

when I wake I rage and prowl filled with unbridled fury that things have turned out so badly for me. I hate myself but I hate this world and this life more. Sometimes in my despair I wish I could end my life; why I don't I do not know since there is nothing to live for. I may not write again, so goodbye."

Every letter ended that way and there never was a return address. So it was until he wrote no more and he said a final goodbye to the world beyond a great fenced off mansion.

CHAPTER 5

THE MANSION OF DESPAIR, HOPE, LIFE, & DEATH

Inside, the mansion was beautiful. There were luxurious drapes and curtains, magnificent chandeliers, tables, chairs, polished floors, clocks, lamps, carpets, paintings, wood-paneling, a huge music-room with instruments of every kind, a massive library with thousands of leather-bound and embossed volumes; there was room after room after room, fully furnished; there were beds, statues, candlesticks, fireplaces; there was oak and mahogany everywhere and there were comfortable little sitting rooms with all that was needed for quiet reflection. Beautiful things, beautiful shapes and frames that only reminded him of the creature in the mirror. Sometimes madness lit torches and threatened to burn the entire place down around the creature and put an end to it all but something—he knew not what—conquered the fury, the fireplaces housed the burning torches and guttural weary sobbing was the only sound in the silent house.

The building on the outside was neglected, lonely-looking and in some ways forbidding. There were large damp patches where fungus grew, there were segments of guttering badly in need of repair and others were choked with weeds. There were windows like soulless eyes that saw nothing but continued to gaze. The area immediately around the house was large and had trees of various kinds that once would have looked beautiful but now were feeble, weary and leaning like aged people as they walk; the fruit trees were fruitless. The entire area was overgrown; dull yellow, faded green, brown and gray were the dominant colors. The entire scene was all sadness and fatigue, a visible low moan.

It might be supposed that the Beast would sink into a kind of peace that hopelessness brings to some people we hear of. They never had anything, they do not now have anything and they have no reason to believe that they ever will so they adapt to their various forms of destitution and deprivation. There was the *Prisoner of Chillon*, years alone in his gloomy cell after the death of his brother, his fellow-prisoner and now buried beneath the floor; alone with his now old friends the cockroaches, mice and other such things. Content finally with the prison walls and door; content with morsels of food silently passed through a vent; content until that fateful day we now imagine when on a whim he succeeded in the extremely difficult climb to a solitary window so high above him. And for a moment or two he saw through it a blue sky, free and graceful birds, white fluffy clouds, dancing waves and a line of tidy little houses on land not too far away.

Strength now gone he slips and slides and tumbles back down into what is now no longer a home, but a coffin, suffocating him. Now he beats and pounds on the iron door, sobbing, "Let me out! Let me out!" Before the imagined climb he had come, Byron tells us, "to love despair." Should he not have climbed? Would it have been better for him not to have seen, to come to know, to want? Many ancient Greeks believed that "hope" was left in Pandora's jar to torment humans; better to resign to fate and adjust to it. Interesting questions but the Beast of our story while he raged and sobbed was kept from total despair and utter hopelessness by what seemed a miracle.

There was a patch of miracle situated at the edge of the path that led from the fence to the door of the great house. A miracle! For there, inexplicably and astonishingly, grew a small patch of truly beautiful roses that never failed to return in a glorious resurrection from among the dead and dying! Many were soft white and others, redder than red, all alive with life and with an aroma that fought the dampness and deadness of all around them. Here was defiance of the most wondrous kind; happy, singing, smiling, swaying, conquering defiance that said no to the sad, wearied and life-denying clutter all around and they gave their voice to another message. It was these defiant, beautiful and fragrant flowers that kept the creature from adding *utter* and unrelieved gloom to his characteristic fury. It was these fragile, vulnerable witnesses to beauty in the middle of death and dying that insisted on living! They should not have been there—but they were! In their weakness they should not have survived— but they did! They didn't apologize for being; they didn't ask permission to live and sway and breathe or to send their lovely fragrance into the sour air all around them!

It's true, his grand house was filled with those real treasures, music rooms with silent musical instruments, unread first-edition books in the vast library, rooms filled with lavish furniture, golden candlesticks, paintings, sculptured pieces, jeweled crosses, necklaces, bracelets and rings and gold coins everywhere but it was the roses that gave him joy—passing perhaps, but real. It was those roses, the living, cheerfully stubborn roses that kept him from a leap into oblivion so it was no wonder he would visit them often. Of all the things he owned these were his almost sacred possession. And on a day when the breeze was right they filled many rooms with their fragrance and spoke to the disfigured creature of beauty in the midst of ugliness, of life in the midst of death. At very critical moments when fear and harsh reality whispered from a solitary mirror, "This is how it ends," through an open window came the aroma that said, "Disease and weariness tell only half a story. Hope against hope. Never cease to believe and you will see!" The roses led the Beast to believe that if they could live while surrounded by despair so could he. No wonder spring was his favorite time of the year; no wonder the roses were more than pretty flowers. It was the roses that explained the torches that burned themselves out in the fireplace rather than becoming part of an inferno that devoured his house and his life.

CHAPTER 6

THE STORM

As he was leaving again her father had kissed her and said, "I shouldn't be away more than two weeks, my dear but don't be worrying if it takes longer than that."

She was tearful. "I will miss you terribly, Papa, you will take care of yourself, won't you?! And bring me a rose if you can."

"I won't forget the rose. And try not to worry about me," he said, as he got on his horse and headed out toward one of the larger towns something like three days ride toward the north. Well into his journey he was weary. Thoughts of failure were dominant knowing that if he failed again things at home would have reached crisis point.

By now he was well into the forest and if he was careful the trails would eventually lead him to where he wanted to go. Then the storm hit—the worst storm in living memory. The winds howled and toppled trees, the rain came down in torrents, visibility was close to nothing, the ground soggy, the lightning splitting trees, various animals in panic. Wheeling and fleeing in all directions and the thunder frightening does into giving birth. His horse bolted with him on it and couldn't be stopped, driven by fear, blindly rushing who knew in what direction and before long it threw his clinging rider and careered on to somewhere with wild eyes filled with terror. Any food remaining went with the tormented animal. He groaned, shivered, prayed and crawled to the strongest tree nearby looking for safety while the heavens made war with the earth. It was dark when many hours later the thunder finally became a mutter in the distance. Disoriented he had no idea where he was as he trembled the hours away until the dawn and then stumbled for nearly a day with no idea in what direction. He was confused, sometimes weeping, sometimes delirious and hungrier than he could ever remember being.

Then he saw the mansion! He began to sob in relief and then in dismay when he realized there was the strong fence and then with more relief when he saw a gap in it. Too desperate to think of any consequences of trespassing he knew he would crawl through, go to the door tell his sad tale and surely the lord of the manor would be sympathetic and kind. He had no choice and soon he was through the fence and making his way to the door while blood-red and bestial eyes watched his approach through a curtained window. He passed roses that were so beautiful that even in his desperation he stopped for a few seconds, startled by their beauty and he thought of his beloved Beatrice. The heavy curtain muffled a growl from the watcher behind it. The desperate traveler beat on the huge solid oak door then leaned on it in his weariness and felt it open. He waited for a moment, heard nothing and entered, shouting apologies as he entered before walking farther into the hall that led to other places. The silence was forbidding and his fear led him back to the door that he now found shut and that's when he heard a voice without a speaker, harsh and resonant, demanding to know why he dared to trespass on private land.

CHAPTER 7

THE MEETING

Henry poured out his tale of woe, to the voice, telling where he had been heading, the search for financial backing due to financial misfortune, his needy family, his dear Beatrice, the storm, the horse, his being lost, his bruises and aches, his hunger and his profound apology for being so presumptuous as to come through the fence. He talked a long time and would have gone on but the voice thundered, "Enough!" and from behind a heavy curtain stepped the most hideous figure the wanderer could have imagined. An almost upright werewolf or some such creature with blood-red eyes that burned into his own. Henry cowered screamed out, "Oh please, please I didn't mean…" The creature silenced him with a savage command, "Be quiet! I am not going to eat you." The man, fatigued, drained, could take no more and he staggered back and collapsed into a huge chair behind him and there he lay.

How long he had been unconscious he didn't know but when he wakened the monster was gone, the table close by was laden with food of all kinds and beside it a scrawled note saying, "Eat, find decent clothes and all you need in one of the bedrooms. Tomorrow you will answer to me!" Henry ate and drank his fill, even while he kept looking over his shoulder and around; he found one of the many bedrooms that served his purposes and finally exhaustion got its way and he fell asleep.

The next morning there on the table was a marvelous breakfast with the instruction, "Eat!" He wolfed the breakfast down despite his nervousness. Then what he feared happened; the beast appeared at the top of a flight of stairs and the traveler stopped eating, his mouth full of food. "Close your mouth you fool and swallow that food or I might change my mind and swallow you," the creature snarled. Speechless the man could only stare. Even after finishing the breakfast Henry Pearson was speechless until the Beast thundered, "Speak! I said we'd speak. Explain more!" and with that the stammering Henry told his once happy now sad story, apologizing repeatedly until the creature hoarsely bellowed, pounding the table. "Stop bleating. You're here! Tell me more about your family."

He told of his wife, his marvelous children and especially of his youngest and sweetest, Beatrice. Not even his fear could mask his obvious love of his family and the as yet unmarried daughter who waited for his safe return. Henry couldn't have known it but he wasn't the only one hungry—the creature was too. Hungry for human company and conversation, hungry for contact with a world he missed beyond the power of words to tell.

"Business! Tell me more of your business." Experienced and wise in business as he had always been Henry spoke at length of his investments, his adequate and steady income and then the series of events over which he had no control that led to bank-loans and interest and an inevitable downward spiral. The creature seemed interested, maybe even understanding — was that it? Did he seem understanding? The intruder wondered to himself. There was nothing friendly about the one before him but while they talked the man sensed an easing of tension and threat. "We'll speak again in the morning," growled the Beast and whirled away and up the wide staircase.

Further days came and went and they were spent in questions and answers, family life, joys and challenges, the nature of the children, what mattered greatly or was of no account—all the responses coming from the traveler and the questions from the fearsome one who breathed noisily and listened intently. Some days later the stream of questions became a trickle and the silences grew longer. Another breakfast alone, with Pearson wondering how it was that the food came to be provided as it was, wondering too how he was to react when the creature appeared. Should he thank him, excuse himself and leave? Would the Beast *allow* him to leave? And when he did leave, what on earth was he to do? The answer came soon when the creature made his appearance.

CHAPTER 8

THE LEAVING, THE OFFENSE & THE AGREEMENT

"In a few hours you will find two horses outside waiting for you, there will be food and other things on one of them. You will go straight home to that daughter of yours and you will have no reason to worry about debt or loans ever again. Now go! Touch nothing and never return!"

Stumbling thanks laced with relief and Henry Pearson hurried out of the giant door that closed behind him and there they were, two horses; one of them large and very strong and strapped to it were numerous bulging bags that he couldn't keep from examining. Shock, bewilderment, astonishment, joy—all these registered with speed as he saw jewels, silver and gold coins—the bags were filled with such wealth as he could never have imagined in his most fevered dreams. From behind the same thick curtain the creature watched the man and saw his look of incredulity and watched him as he turned to look at the house, unsure if he should come to thank the hideous-looking benefactor. He watched until the man decided it was best to do what he was told and go! As he slowly made his way over the clearing toward the gate of the fence, delirious with joy, he thought of his beloved daughter and then remembered her last words to him; "Bring me back a lovely rose if you are able." He stopped, got off the horse and walked eagerly to the roses and swiftly gathered a number of them.

Immediately a howling, the giant door flew open, the lurching screaming thing ran right at him; words came like a torrent from his misshapen mouth but they carried only one message. "You heartless thief! You thankless robber! You presumptuous, sly and greedy wretch; you would steal my very life?" The Beast with teeth bared was now shaking the man violently and Death made his appearance and waited nearby.

"The roses, sir?" he gasped as he choked, "They were for Beatrice, sir. I meant no harm. They were for my beautiful Beatrice. I thought since you had been so generous that some roses would have meant nothing to you." All this he had to struggle to get out while the Beast raged and screamed and threatened and grasped. "You will die for this. I gave you the treasure as a gift but you, a contemptible thief would steal what matters most to me."

The man whimpered, "I did not think they meant so much to you, sir."

The creature exploded, more angry still, "Who gave you the right to make such a judgment. I *will* take your life."

Henry begged for his own sake but even more fervently for sweet Beatrice's sake, saying how she would die of heartbreak and loneliness if he never returned. "She loves me even more than I love her if that's possible," he sobbed as he struggled for air.

"She means that much to you?" screamed the incensed creature, easing his grasp on the man's throat. "How would you feel if I stole her from you as you have stolen from me?"

"Oh, please, she is all I have to make life bearable and I am all she has—she will die."

"And my roses," the Beast hissed, "is all I have to make living bearable and you put forth your vile hands and would have stolen them from me."

Struggling still to speak the man said, "I did not know, sir. Had I known I would not have rewarded your kindness by stealing from you. I meant no offense. It was not greed, sir, that made me take your beautiful roses but a father's deep and eager love of one who means more to him than life itself. If you only knew her, sir, and how the very thought of her fills me with joy; joy because of our love for each other. If you could know how she has longed for roses in her own little garden which has none, you could perhaps be able to forgive me this great wrong. It was the image of her face and her delight when she would see your roses—not ordinary roses, but the loveliest roses I have ever seen or heard of in all my travels. Their incomparable beauty and my love for her blinded me to the courtesy of asking. She would be as overcome as I am by the wealth you have poured out on us both and what it means to those we owe so much as well as to our own honor in repaying honorable debts. But it would be the roses that she would immediately dance with joy and sing about."

As he spoke these words the Beast became quiet and then released his grip and Death who had lingered close moved farther away. Almost quietly the horrible creature asked, "She would love my roses that much?"

"Yes, sir," Henry gasped, "more than I can express. As I left her last words were not about business success or my restored honor but about a rose."

"And what would she think of someone who gave her a gift of such roses?"

"She would feel indebted to him all her life, sir. She would not know how to repay such kindness and generosity."

Suddenly, fierce again, the creature yelled, "Are you lying to me to save your miserable life? You must speak the truth to me. You must not lie! Would she truly love my roses that much? Would she feel so indebted to someone…" (the speech slowed and became almost hushed) "even if he looked like me?" The tone now almost a wish.

"I do not lie to you. I tell you again, her last words to me as I left to come this way were, 'Bring me back a rose if you can'."

"And does she love you as much as you say?"

"She does. In a heartbeat she would gladly give her life for me. Anything honorable, no matter what it cost, she would do for me as I for her," the man said.

"I must meet her," said the creature. "And I will let you go if you will agree to have her come to live here with me. Would she do that for you or are you like all the self-seekers who agree and flatter and speak lies to get from me what they want?" (Then face to the sky, roaring) "Like everyone I have ever known in a world filled with flatterers? Is there no truth or goodness to be found? Is there even one genuine person I can turn to?"

(Slowly, the still-cowering man) "She would do that for me if I were to ask her. Not only would she die for me, she would live for me as she has always done."

"And will you ask her and allow her to come?"

(Even more slowly, thoughtfully, and then,) "Would you ever harm her? You want truth *from* me—speak it *to* me. If I thought you would harm her I would gladly die, here and now without regret."

"I would never harm her," said the creature.

"What if I agreed and then did not ask her?" said the man.

"I would find you if I had to search the world over," the creature hissed. "But *are* you the kind who gives his word and keeps it or are you the liar I could easily think you are?"

"If I gave you my word I would live and die by it," the man said, "and are you one who would keep his word that you would never harm my daughter?"

"I am!"

"How long would you compel her to stay with you?"

"As long as I choose. The decision will be mine and you will never return here but you can be sure I will never harm her."

"Forgive me if you can or feel you must if I offend you," said the man, "but you must know that your appearance is frightening and those who frighten us are difficult to trust."

"If I were handsome would you trust me more easily?"

"I have known handsome and beautiful people whose words were poison and lies. That I know! I only say that as foolish it is, we expect truth and trustworthiness to be linked to a fine face and a normal appearance. However it has come to be, we link ugliness or beastliness with what is sinister and dangerous. Assure me, I beg you, that my sweet daughter would be safe with you."

"I am not a beast," the man-beast screamed, "I'm a man that cannot get free from this curse that alienates me from myself and from life itself."

"Look at me," said the anxious father, "and tell me again, please, that you will never harm her."

Now calmed and now moved by the anxious love before him, the imprisoned man-beast quietly said, "She would be safe with me. I would never harm her nor would I ever let harm come to her."

"Then I will go home and ask her to come."

"You will *ask* her to come?"

"I won't need to *tell* her. For love of me and the family she will choose to come whatever the hardship. I have no idea why you have been generous beyond words to me and mine. You have given me your word that you will protect and care for my precious daughter. I will entrust her to you. Please, tell me once more that you will protect her from harm."

"I will not," the man-beast said. "Believe me. If I lied to you once I would lie to you again if it suited me. I will send transport for your daughter on this day six weeks from now. See you *keep* your word or you and your whole family will suffer the consequences."

Anxious now to leave the man left with this "There *are* those in the world who keep their word and I am one of them. If you are trustworthy be assured that I am."

"Six weeks from today," growled the creature.

CHAPTER 9

THE RETURN, THE STORY & THE DEPARTURE

Henry's return spread through the district as fast as lightning fills the night sky. Rumors multiplied and stories were told by those that had caught a glimpse of his reappearance. The next day the locals gawked, whispered and watched until the last member of the Pearson family had made its way to the modest little house just off from Francis Street.

The gathered children were dumbstruck when they saw the treasure that flowed from some of the large sacks that were opened. The hard-to-believe story was told. They conferred for several days. Maybe, to keep Beatrice with them they could flee for with such wealth they could hide, change their names; they could do whatever it took to remain hidden. No, the father said, for anyone who could part with such wealth as if it were nothing must have unimaginable wealth and power. He would find them. There was nothing for it, for love of her father and her family she would go. In any case, Henry Ellison Pearson had given his word to someone who had redeemed the family from public shame as well as looming abject poverty. And in doing this *he* had saved Beatrice also and who knew what loveliness the future might hold for the girl? Must the awful appearance of the benefactor be the only reality—must his unprovoked generosity and his word count for nothing?

In all the discussion there was that in the mind of Beatrice that she never mentioned. The family was now free—more than free—from financial difficulties forever, their love for one another was as deep and true as ever it would be, her honorable and generous father was back in business; all was well at home!

Though she hid it, Beatrice felt a growing excitement. She was young, alive, loved, and had never been away from home. The creature might be ugly but he cannot have been as grotesque as her father had said and in any case her father's judgment and the creature's astounding generosity weighed heavily with her. The siblings spoke their goodbyes to each other, again and again, and Beatrice spoke in private to her sorrowful father confessing her excitement.

One morning of the day appointed by the mysterious benefactor they found a grand carriage in the street outside the house. The coachman would answer no questions. All that was needed for the trip was stored in the coach. There was more hugging, more tears and there were goodbyes from neighbors wishing her the best and away she went—a ransom.

CHAPTER 10

BEATRICE & THE BEAST

The gate was opened and so was the great door to the house but she saw no sign of the creature her father had described. There was food on the table and a note saying "EAT" and telling her she was to do as she wished in any of the many rooms and bedrooms. She was hungry and should have been tired but being very nervous and excited she ate little.

From there she began to explore the rooms, none of which were locked and all of them were fitting for such a mansion. She entered a large, high-ceilinged room that was nevertheless comfortable. It had a huge fireplace and the kinds of chairs that poor people dreamed of. High up on a strong but fancy perch sat the statue of a giant white parrot. Beatrice gazed long at it and then turned to admire other things when the voice rang out, "Who are you? Why are you here?" The girl jumped with fright and wheeled around and the parrot screamed out, "You're a monster!" Mirror, mirror, on the wall, who's the ugliest of all? You!" Then silence.

Beatrice soon recovered and spoke to the parrot. "We're you speaking to me? I wouldn't have thought someone as beautiful as you would be so rude and insulting." The parrot stared in silence and the girl said, "You are beautiful you know and you should speak sweet things." The parrot suddenly bellowed in a guttural voice, "I'm hideous! Can't you see? Who are you? Leave this house at once!"

"But I've been invited here," Beatrice said.

"Well, then, I suppose you can stay. But leave soon, and that's my last word." He buried his huge head in his huge chest and went to sleep.

The excitement and edginess diminished and weariness took over. She found her way to a beautiful bedroom but it wouldn't have mattered if it had been a run-down hostel, it had a bed and she was exhausted so it wasn't long before she was fast asleep in this strange place.

A few days slipped by and now and then from some distant part of the house she would hear crashing and breaking sounds as though things were being thrown and wrecked and there were fearful guttural growls or screaming—a great wild animal sending out a challenge to something somewhere. And at other times, late in the night she heard the mournful cries of a lost soul, pleading, imploring, saying things she could not hear well. She heard the anguished, "Why?" ring out from time to time.

CHAPTER 11

THROUGH A DOOR DARKLY

Beatrice once more made a round of the rooms and checked the many she hadn't seen. She tried all the doors of the house for there were no signs to forbid it and none of them was ever locked. That was true until one early evening she tried to enter one room at the end of a long corridor and found the door locked. She tried it again, then paused, for she thought she heard movement. "Hello?" she said and since there was no response she tried once more and a thunderous voice that shook the door panels cried, "Go Away!" Frightened beyond measure she ran to her room, listened for a long time afraid of the approach of the fearful creature with the awful voice and terrible rage. There was no sound, the fear subsided enough to allow her to sob for her father and for home. This went on for much of the night though for a little while she dreamed of a handsome young man that talked gently to her, soothingly, and telling her—she didn't know why—not to trust appearances too much for while they often told truth they didn't tell all the truth and sometimes they even lied. And now and then she dreamed conflicting things about hideous faces and sacks of golden coins and laughter, of giant parrots screaming "ugliness" and fatherly comfort and assurance.

The next morning after a cautious walk to the table there was her delicious breakfast and a scrawled note. "I'm sorry I frightened you. I listened to you crying in the night for the father that loves you. How deeply you must love him to be willing to live in this awful place for his sake. I'm sorry. Come again."

But the shock and the fear remained vivid and she did not dare return to that door until one morning several days later, another scrawled note. "I am truly sorry. *Please* come again." She thought about it for another day and after a perfect lunch and dinner she found her way to that door again, knocked and tried the handle.

"It's locked," (a voice, flat and guttural.)

"But you told me to come. I will go away now."

"Don't go away." (the same voice) "The door is locked for your benefit."

"Ohhh! You mean you might hurt me?"

"I would never hurt you but you wouldn't want to see me. I would frighten you...I look so... I would frighten anyone. I frighten even myself sometimes. Speak to me through the door."

"I don't know what to talk about."

"Talk about anything. Just hearing your voice, any voice, is wonderful." (softer the creature half quietly growled)

"Please," why are you so ugly?"

"Because I am!" (snarled the voice through the door)

"I'm sorry." (frightened, stepping away from the door) "I meant to say, why is it that you are this way; the way you say you are?"

There was a long pause—was it that the creature wanted to talk no more? She began to excuse herself and leave but the voice came through the door.

"I've thought about 'why' for several years and I think I have become as I am because I have been so ugly inside for so long. I think somehow that is how it is supposed to be—that someone or something has life arranged that way."

"What do you mean 'ugly on the inside'?"

"I mean vicious, arrogant and heartless." [She could hear the creature pace up and down.] "People were beneath me, weak and ignorant because they weren't rich or well-read or ruthless like me. I wanted more, more money, more power, more recognition; I wanted to be feared. I gained vast wealth and power on the backs of powerless people and I showed others how to do it. I was ugly and I taught others to admire ugly, I made cold-bloodedness fashionable and heartlessness something to be enjoyed. I was surrounded by sycophants and sneered at them and I saw the masses as sheep to be shorn and fed on. I made evil appear good. I am being punished!"

"But, why aren't there millions ugly as you are—I mean—ugly as you say you are?"

"I have no answer for that," (he roared impatiently, pounding on the door and she backing away) "Don't ask me questions I don't have answers for. I only know that is how I have come to see it in *me*. Maybe I'm fate's object lesson to remind others that ugliness within us will work its way out in hideousness and horror."

"But you don't seem ugly inside now. These aren't the words of someone repulsive inside. Though you have frightened me and though I thought you might hurt or kill me you have done me no harm. You sound very sorry for the inner ugliness you speak of. And you are indeed ugly?"

(The voice thundered from behind the door) "I said I was ugly! Didn't I? I need no lectures from you about my ugliness! Will I never be free? (The frustration and anguished rage spilling out) I resent the very idea that I am responsible for……..for *this that I see in the mirror*. The way I lived is the way of the world and I shouldn't be penalized for it (the volume dropping and a softer tone) but then I see the swagger in the beautiful and the powerful and wonder if I really looked like them. (rage again) **Everyone lies! Friends deserted me when….Ahhh…There is no love in the world so why should I have been different?** I resent that others as evil as I have been are not as hideous as I am. But now I regret nothing (he thunders on the door, a pause and volume dropping) and I scream my fury into the night that doesn't care that I came or that I will go and at other times I despise myself for whimpering into the same darkness." (Then bitter last words) "Now leave me! I wish to speak no more."

Beatrice wanted to interrupt, tried, but she heard him move away from the door with deep-sounding groans and so she turned away toward her own room. Sometime later she thought she heard what sounded like weeping and felt a momentary surge of pity for whoever this was that appeared to be two beings in one. That night she dreamed again of the handsome young man and as usual in the dream they spoke of life and love and pleasant things and then a little of the monster in the distant room, alone in his self-hatred. Is she afraid of him now? Does she no longer think him ugly? Is there no such thing as physical beauty? Is physical beauty the main thing? Is there beauty apart from physical beauty? Can the very ugly really be gentle? Could ugly ever become *interesting* rather than sheerly ugly? These questions she wrestled with in her dreams as dreamers do but the physical presence of the repulsive creature who was holding her as ransom destroyed calm reasoning and options—he was or at least *sounded* fiercely and frighteningly ugly! Yet, as time went by familiarity destroyed shock and revulsion and tolerance entered. The horrid one kept an acceptable distance and spoke of the world outside, sometimes longingly, wanting to know about village life, its pleasures and challenges and about her father's business and her brothers and sisters. Beatrice found herself astonished at the power of conversation and how marvelously his genuine interest in her and her life *humanized* this creature.

CHAPTER 12

FACE TO FACE

Weeks went by and she felt very lonely. Books were wonderful, music even more so but without someone to share lovely things with….. She often asked herself why she no longer felt fear even when the creature's rage that reached her ears was so marked and the voice so threatening. Why did she feel she was becoming used to him? Could he, when he spoke words about regret and guilt, could he hate himself so much, could he have been as ugly as his words said he was? If he was not as inwardly ugly as he said he was or had been, perhaps he wasn't as ugly in appearance as he said he was. She wrote him a note and slipped it under his door and hurried away.

"May I *never* see you? Will we *never* speak again? Must I live here all my life and *never* see the one who is providing all I need? Will you not show yourself to me?"

The note she got in return at breakfast the next morning said: "I'm afraid."

The return note to him said, "You? Afraid? How could one like me make one like you afraid?"

"I have come to enjoy your presence here even though we do not speak. Your love for your father that led you to be kept from him without time constraints is something I haven't seen before, something I haven't felt before and you have entered my heart and have changed me somehow."

"But if you think so well of me and if in some way I give you hope why won't you let me see you?"

"Because in foolish and wild thoughts I have even dared to imagine that you might come to like me if you didn't see me. I know for certain that if you saw me—the real me—you would never want to be near me. You simply have no idea how hideous I am! My life now is miserable beyond description even in the midst of all this wealth and beauty but if you saw me and were forever repulsed by me, it would be unendurable. You are not the only one who has taken a colossal risk. If you, being as your father described you and being now as you seem to be—if you should turn forever from me I could not go on living."

(her) "So, you choose to live until one of us dies—two lonely people. Me, lonely for my father and my home and you longing for life; we two sharing one grand house, never speaking and never trusting; two prisoners in a beautiful home that only reminds you of the ugliness you speak of? If I see you and cannot bear you, will you be more alone than you are now? Who knows, perhaps I will not think you as ugly as you think you are. Come, let me see you. Don't be afraid, for I am not."

More notes were exchanged. Some became long letters; the kind that revealed past days of joy and of memories sad and pleasant.

"I heard you sing and play," he said. "It was beautiful even though it was sad."

"And did you sing or play when you were young?"

"I did both. Then before I knew it I was engrossed in business and life became less than life had been. I didn't regret the loss for the new venture was glorious but it stole from me as well as giving to me; and it hardened me in ways that I didn't need to be hard and I became a brute to others.

"That isn't *all* ugly,"

"You don't know and I have no wish to tell you of how callous and under-handed I became and how cruel I was to those who had no power to stand against me. In my cruelty I became a model for those who admired me. Like me they became haughty, swaggering, well-dressed and socially sophisticated they were, nearly as cheap and grubby as I was in my veneer of grandeur. My pleasure in music and friendship slowly disappeared because the adventure and glory in business shut out everything else. I ceased playing and friends were no longer friends. But I confess I loved hearing you. It stirred something in me that I thought was forever and completely dead."

Her next letter said only this: "Come, let me see you."

That evening after dinner a voice said, "Don't turn. I'm here. I'm so afraid to show myself but now I am more afraid not to. Remember, I would never hurt you. I will dim the lights and then you can turn." Her heart trembled and her lips quivered as she slowly turned and there in the darkness near the stairs stood a figure in the shadows. Bracing herself she whispered, "Step out of the shadows, I can't see you clearly." The creature did and the sight of him took her breath away. She screamed but stifled it. Her mind whirled in a barely controlled panic and she wanted to run but fear rooted her to the spot. She stood silent and trembling.

"Say something!" (the thing roared hoarsely and then immediately, in something close to desperate pleading,) **"Anything! Run! Scream some more! Tell me it's too much to bear. Tell me I am what I know myself to be."** It was the anguished tone that saved them both for she stayed.

"Why..." she said holding herself together for them both but lying, "you're...not a real monster...you're...a man. I was still afraid you would be the monster I heard howling and destroying but now you're here, I know I was more afraid of what I imagined you to be. The sound and the fury hid things from me and my vision of you was more frightening than now.

"Am I not hideous?"

"Please don't ask me that, such a question should not be asked or answered. I'm afraid to make you angry and you might hurt me."

"Your refusal to answer is an answer. There must be honesty between us and you must tell me if I am hideous."

"Must we be honest if we must be *heartless* to be honest? Must we worship honesty at the expense of kindness and pity?"

"I don't want your pity," he said, his volume rising, his tone harsher. "Tell me, am I ugly?"

"Yes! You're ugly, very ugly! Hideous"

(A loud, fierce and guttural sound from him and she afraid but fright became defensive)

"What did you expect me to say? You insist I express my feelings and now you frighten me for expressing them. You demanded honesty rather than pity and now you make me tremble for giving you what you demand. Is this your honesty?"

"I must have the truth from you…".

(He begins. She interrupts.)

"Your heartless mirrors will give you all the truth you need. I would have thought you knew that by now. If you want to torment yourself with obvious truths go to your mirror and do not come to me; you will not steal the heart from me in your desire to torture yourself."

(At that moment she remembered he had no mirrors in any of the rooms.)

"But you have no mirrors in this house, do you?"

"I have one," speaking slowly, "In my room."

There was silence for a moment or two, both afraid of breaking it. She was the stronger of the two and took a step toward him and he, still very afraid, took a step back as if to leave.

"Don't go, Please don't go. We're both afraid for different reasons but now I believe that you mean me no harm. I promise you with all my heart I will not knowingly speak to hurt you."

"I must go. Your words overwhelm me. I expected something else and was prepared, perhaps, for the worst but this tenderness is more than I can bear. Goodnight!"

With that he was gone but she called after him,

"What shall I call you? What is your name? I can't call you 'monster'."

His voice echoed down the hall, **"Phillip! I once was known as Phillip."**

"I am Beatrice," she shouted and heard him repeat it before he slammed the door to his room.

CHAPTER 13

A SURPRISE MEETING AND A MYSTERY SOLVED

It was one of those days that we all need now and then and she was walking alone, following a path she hadn't been on before. Another bend, and there before her was a large house in a clearing, some horses in a paddock and behind the house a very large structure something like a barn but grander than that. Beatrice froze, momentarily afraid that she had trespassed into some private property, but then remembered that this entire forest area belonged to her extraordinarily wealthy host. She felt awkward and intrusive and several of the horses added to the feeling by breaking off their activities to stand still and looking long at this stranger as if to ask, "Why are you here?" Nevertheless she walked slowly toward the house calling hello until she saw the front door open slightly and someone looking at her. "Hello," she said, "I am Beatrice. I am a guest at the manor. I hope I'm not trespassing. I didn't know this house was here. I hope you don't think it rude of me." The sentences came out quickly—too quickly—but she did feel intrusive and wanted to explain herself before the door shut. It didn't close, it opened wider and a mature woman and man stepped out to meet the visitor. Once hearts calmed, but still outside the house, they introduced themselves as Mariana from Spain and Lino her husband, from Italy. They had two sons that lived with them. The lovely food that she enjoyed and was delivered every day was made in this house by these two fine people assisted by their grown boys. Fear was now completely gone and they invited her in and she was pleased with their comfortable home but absolutely delighted and a bit amazed at the huge kitchen that would have matched the most finely equipped kitchen of any restaurant anywhere in the world. There were huge freezers and refrigerators, glittering stoves with uncommon options, specially constructed shelves filled with all that could rightly be imagined for such a place. Gleaming pots and pans, sacks of this and that in huge slide-out cupboards and concealed drawers filled with cutlery and bottles of one thing or another. There were vegetables and fruits, there was flour and rice and there was the lingering aroma of bread not long baked. The place was spotless but not like a hospital for there was the smell of fresh things and then there were plates and cups, bowls and dishes, utensils custom-made to ensure that hot food remained hot as long as reason would require and that what should be cold was kept cold. Beatrice reflecting on the wonderful meals she had been enjoying, praised and thanked these people. A door disguised as part of a paneled wall near the dining area led to a long corridor that became the entrance to and the exit from the house; the mystery of the appearing food and the disappearing remainders was solved. These two master cooks and bakers were a match for their amazing kitchen.

"How long have you worked for him?" Beatrice asked while drinking some wine and eating a freshly baked scone. "We've known the master of the manor for many years," Lino said, "but he only called us to come here about six years ago." Mariana quickly added, "But we haven't seen him for many years. He will not permit us to meet with him here. Have you seen him?" Beatrice did not feel free to say much and so she evaded the question. "I have heard him move about upstairs him and spoken to him through a door but he must have some good reason to hide away. I have heard of people who prefer complete seclusion. But I haven't been here as long as you, perhaps I will see him by and by. I know that my father has met him and that he has been extraordinarily generous to him."

"Well," said Mariana, we both know about his generosity. He is unbelievably generous to us. Would you say that for us if you are speaking to him again?" Lino nodded vigorously in agreement, "There's no way to understand what he has done for us. It beggars description."

"How does he communicate with you?" Beatrice was curious to know and Lino said, "We have a place we check regularly for notes." And then, a little nervously he said, "But understand, now and then we're gone from here and the master of the manor has forbidden us to speak to anyone about our business or our home here. The truth is, we're a little nervous about speaking to you and did not expect to ever meet anyone here." Beatrice got the message and responded quickly. "Of course! He prizes his privacy beyond everything else and since we are blessed by his kindness it would be terrible to speak of our place and situation here. If I should happen to be speaking to him again I would make known to him that you fully understand that and are happy beyond measure to continue to abide by his wishes. It is probably best for me to tell him we have met and that it was completely by accident. Be assured that no word of mine about our meeting would get you in trouble. This has been a very pleasing visit with you and I am grateful for your hospitality." Best wishes were spoken, mutual pleasure was expressed at the happy meeting and Beatrice returned the way she came.

CHAPTER 14

DREAMS AND QUESTIONS

Knowing the worst was over between her and the lord of the manor she quietly made her way to the stairs that led to his room and listened to his soft weeping—weeping that lacked the anguish she had become familiar with. Gone too was the howling and screaming—she heard no more of that ever again.

Weeks became months! Walks in the forest and horseback riding there made the days pass by quickly. Now and then she would look at the monster and think that he didn't look just as cruelly ugly as when she first came to this place of exile but she was content to believe he hadn't changed—she was simply no longer utterly repelled by his looks. Yes, that was it, she'd grown accustomed to him; there was no change in him; the change was in her! She had experienced that before through the years. And yet, she couldn't quite shake the thought that his eyes were not just as frighteningly red, his facial hideousness was not quite as marked. But no, it wasn't him, it was her.

"I know I repulse you," he said to her one day, right out of the blue. "but there is nothing I can do about it."

"I wish to say no more about your appearance than this. You look as you look and that is real but there are other things that are just as real; maybe even more real because they remain when other things go away. One day I will be old and wrinkled and ugly..." He interrupted and assured her that she would never be ugly—

"You are beautiful,"

"I am not at all *beautiful*. I have two sisters who are beautiful. I will not ever be beautiful but I am not as ugly as some ...I...have...seen." The sentence dragged off and she put her hand over her mouth, began to apologize

"You mean not as ugly as I am?"

She began to explain but his response at her embarrassment finally conquered and silenced her. She recovered, relaxed and smiled.

"You are beautiful to me, Beatrice..." (she interrupts to deny it but he responds)

"You mustn't forbid me to express what my heart feels. If you can understand why people would think me ugly you mustn't silence me if I sincerely think you beautiful—and I do. In these past months I have seen a loveliness that affects how I see what I see with my eyes. Remember that I have seen only awful ugliness for so long and if you silence me you rob me of joy I haven't known for years." (her muted protests died when she realized he had a point and it was selfish to rob him of whatever pleasure he found in her as a new friend)

Yessssss." (she whispered slowly and then...) "I will not say that ugliness is beauty — within or outwardly, but neither will I say that appearance is everything. The level of your disfigurement has robbed you, and still does, of friends and praise and open involvement with many lovely things in life. Now that I know I have nothing to fear I will not rob you of whatever joy my friendship and presence might bring."

"When I had freedom unlimited," he said, "I was a fool, a heartless, arrogant fool that worshiped appearance." (hissing bitterly, pausing, and then sadly) "If I had known more people like you perhaps I would have been a better person. I realize that's no excuse for..." (she interrupts)

"I hear no excuses. (gently) Cruelty is cruelty however we explain it or wherever we find it, but you too, whoever you were before you came to live behind these walls alone, loving no one, and unloved—you too were shaped by the world we live in. It's another kind of fool that denies we are shaped by the powerful forces all around us."

"But would you not rather that I were handsome?"

"Of course I would, but for more than one reason and perhaps more for you than for me now that I am no longer afraid of you and now that I have become used to seeing you. I never thought I would hear myself say this with complete sincerity, but if I were forced to choose between extreme physical misshapenness and appalling deformity of heart and mind I would choose the physical. I have no fear of you at all and I am becoming accustomed to your appearance. Had you been as profoundly corrupt and corrupting within as you are hurt on the outside, my father would have died here on your land before permitting us to meet.

The beast-man groaned. "Yes, my dear, but you cannot know the agony and anguish of this condition. You walk away from what you see but I am repulsed by everything I see and cannot close my eyes or mind to."

"You're right of course. It's easy for me to make choices when I don't have to make those choices. I only wish to make the point that I'd rather be one murdered than have the evil and vicious heart that would murder. I *do* know that I'm making choices that are no actual choices but I can't deny what my heart says. I have come to know something of the you within and that 'you' is filled with redeeming thoughts and feelings. Now that I am coming to know you I am glad we met and I would regret the loss of our friendship."

And so the friendship developed, slowly. She contentedly pretending to be more at peace than she was, stealing glances at the horror who kept company with her. Breakfasts, lunches and dinners together, long conversations and long walks in the huge garden, admiring the happy roses and taking pleasure in horse-riding in forest trails. Weeks became months, leaves turned from green to gold and back, snow covered the earth with a blanket of quietness and then the warm sun returned and life returned in fullness and she now had no difficulty whatever in understanding every word he spoke from that painfully hurt mouth.

CHAPTER 15

JOY & PAIN: THE GRAND AFFAIR REVISITED

And so the slow adjustment to the presence of the other was left behind and mutual respect and laughter became common—her giggling and his happy sounds. They had talked enough about his appearance and there was no more need to explain or justify anything. Together they became swans and there was no more an ugly duckling— just two close and happy friends.

He would tell things against himself from time to time but no longer in that deeply burdened way that the guilty often suffer from without relief. In some way her enjoying his friendship gave him permission to speak of himself without the customary verbal self-rape. Now the confessions were more just the part of his autobiography; not always enjoyed but genuinely confessional. He spoke of places he had been privileged to see and people he was blessed to meet, exotic food he got to sample strange customs he had watched in far off lands, islands and beautiful lagoons he had visited on his luxurious yacht. Beatrice was a great audience to his sad confessions and his thrilled reminisces.

"I enjoyed looking at myself in the mirrors, with the lights well-placed to show me at my best, admiring my good looks and fine body and the flattering clothes especially tailored for me— clothes that I knew would start a fashion when I paraded and strutted before the celebrated ones. How I loved to hear them oooh and ahh about my appearance. If they could see me now, eh?" He made a sound only she would have recognized.

"Phillip, did you just chuckle at that?" Beatrice asked him. He raised his eyes skyward and dismissed her question with a wave of his hairy, gnarled hand. "You did!" she laughed, He waved dismissively again. "But you did!" she insisted, still laughing. "Now there's a stunning first!" Perhaps he smiled but who could tell but himself?

"Anyway, to be invited to my gatherings in any one of my magnificent mansions was what people prayed for. To be seen standing even close to me was a social triumph. Only the most prominent and sophisticated in dress and social graces were invited. The music was the best, the food was prepared by famous chefs, served at grand tables by the best dressed and politest servants. Nothing was allowed to spoil these gala occasions—my glory and reputation were at stake. Mistakes were never tolerated and people were humiliated and dismissed. Heavens, how I loved it and lived for it. Underneath all that appeared to be generous was self-adoration and the wealth that funded all those occasions was gained by merciless business practices that destroyed the business and lives of countless honest companies that were a blessings to thousands of employees I cared nothing about."

There was no fierce self-denunciation now as he spoke of himself in this way. Nor did he speak of it as if it were something to be proud of. He found it somehow liberating to confess to her, believing that if she could forgive him of his awful appearance that she could and would forgive him of what had been within.

"The staff must have lived in fear of such occasions and so must the visitors who came. Perfection can be a ruthless tyrant." The remark was perhaps tactless but his response showed he took no offense.

"Yes, but **I** was the tyrant. I never failed to dismiss hard-working people for the flimsiest reasons and sometimes with no reason at all because the entire thing did not give me the emotional satisfaction I thought it should. I didn't always do it quietly. I remember once dismissing more than fifty men and women after one of the gatherings.

"Oh dear. Poor people. And the excuse for that?"

"I didn't need or offer excuses; not me! Not the grand one. I did such things so often that it came to be expected. But this I remember well and I don't know why it has stayed so long with me and so clearly. The voice dropped to softer tone as he said, "A young woman turned up in what I suppose was her Sunday best dress, neat and acceptable, I suppose. She simply didn't belong. She was pretty but no breathtaking beauty and she didn't have the social graces; she didn't know how to carry herself, she was bewildered and…she simply didn't belong in the company I kept. My face burned with embarrassment. Once she was pointed out to me I saw her trying to make conversation with various ones and saw their amazement and watched them walk off.

"Poor thing. How very painful for her."

"Poor thing indeed; but why didn't she leave immediately? She had to know she didn't belong in such a place with such fine people. She was obviously a village or town girl."

"I wonder why she came," said his companion, "and how she got in without being invited?"

"But that's just it—she had an invitation. Somehow, and I never learned how, one must have been delivered to her."

"Well that would explain it. For people like you an invitation is an invitation but for people like her an invitation is like a command. *Not* to come would be thought an insult to the host. Her heart must have been choking her as she approached the mansion. So what happened then? What did 'his majesty' do about the girl who cheapened his glorious occasion?" (Her tone now flatter as a realization grew)

"His majesty behaved like the beast he was. He collared his chief footman tongue-lashed him before his peers and dismissed him with a kick and all of that despite his polite protests that she had an invitation, which he was attempting to show to me."

"And then what happened to the girl?" The tone was now flat. "Did she attempt to defend the poor man?"

"She did, but I pushed her out of the way with hardly a look. I wasn't prepared to bandy words with her…though it did occur to me that she *did* have an invitation. My pride required me at least to feed her. But I certainly wasn't going to seat her at one of the grand tables and subject my guests to the humiliation of her presence. So…

"That's when you had one of your servants drag her by the arm into the kitchen and set her down in a corner with a plate of food in her lap?"

"Yes…but how did you know that?"

"Because it was one of the most painful moments of my life; one that I knew I would remember all my life."

He was stunned, hesitant, stammering. "It was you? You were the girl?"

"I was! So you were the handsome monster that for so long turned many of my dreams into nightmares—dreams I woke from with trembling and sobs. I can now tell you that I much prefer your current consummate ugliness to your hideous handsomeness then."

With that, his confessor walked off to her room, choking back the rage with the tears and the pain of a newly opened wound. Days followed, silent days, the silence only broken by mournful sounds that from time to time echoed through the halls and corridors. By and by, glances, good mornings and other social conventions melted the freeze and conversation began like a trickle that became a stream. Resentment in one and felt shame in the other finally lost out to the hunger for human friendship. In her response Beatrice learned something about herself and something about deeply buried, even forgotten, anger and resentment that can quickly smolder and then burst into flame. Then bitter alienation, lost friendship and the consequences of such a great loss.

"Will you forgive me for my bitterness and childish resentment?"

"Will you forgive me for my abominable treatment of you and the poor man you defended?"

In the course of ridding themselves of inner hurt she apologized to him and he poured out his sadness that he had so treated her. He vowed he would somehow find the man he had mistreated and make everything right. They sat looking at one another and understood even more clearly that friendship completely revisions an act or a word. Had he known her as he now knew her the entire incident never would have happened no matter how rich and famous he had been. He now knew he would have lived in a house next door to her in a village street and felt happy about it.

CHAPTER 16

LOVE SHARED & LOVE UNREQUITED

"Isn't this a wonderful day?" said he.

What do you mean? said she.

"I mean the sky's blue, the grass is green and we are friends."

Smiling she said, "I knew what you meant; I just wanted to hear you say it. Yes it is a glorious day and our friendship gives it some of its glory."

"I don't wish to go on and on about this, my dear Beatrice, but do you now think me as ugly as I am? I don't *feel* as ugly since I've been around you. Sometimes you look at me and I forget how I look for I see no sign of reluctance or *distance* in your glance. More often now you look more directly at me when you speak and I think, I like to think, you are forgetting my appearance."

"I have grown accustomed to you, Phillip," she said, "and the disfigurement doesn't distress me as it did. Do I see it? Of course I do but I ceased long ago linking your appearance with the thought that you are a monster and that made all the difference. Your appearance is no longer a wall between us."

She said no more about that point but it had occurred to her again, as it had done earlier that there was some improvement in his appearance, his way of carrying himself, something about his overall demeanor but then again on consideration she thought it was only his growing happiness. She was seeing his pleasure and the harshness of his speech was not just as pronounced because she had become familiar to it. She several times thought of mentioning it but was afraid it might raise hope in him that would never be fulfilled.

But he pressed the matter, trying to be lighthearted as if it didn't matter much but failing at that. "Do you think you could ever see me as if I weren't this way?

"I can't answer such a question, Phillip, but I know that from my perspective your appearance has become totally irrelevant. *You* are now who I see! Who knows what can happen. Had you asked in the early days if I could ever become accustomed to your appearance I would have said the question was absurd—of course I could not, and yet here we are, really good friends."

There was silence and then softly he said, "I don't suppose we could ever become more than friends, could we my dear? Do you think you ever could come to love me?" But then quickly, before she could respond, "I know it's ridiculous to say such a thing and I only ask because I have come to love you and because I can no longer keep it to myself. Like a teenage boy I find myself telling it to the trees and the deer, I think they look but they don't understand. I told it to Schubert; he winked at me and then stuck his head back under his wing. I tell it to the stars outside my window every night and for weeks I've been whispering it to you every time your back is to me and once you turned asked me if I was speaking to you and I said I wasn't, it was just my breathing—I lied. I shouldn't expect and I wouldn't even dare to ask such a thing if you had not been so wonderful, forgiving, understanding and beautiful in your graciousness. I tell my mirror that I'm a lunatic to even daydream such things but the fault is partly yours... your way and your gentleness...you've...wakened feelings and longings which I thought had long died in me. You've driven from me wicked emotions of resentment and fury, you have calmed and gentled me and made me already a better man who wishes to be even better. You make we wish

I had never been as I was. It's thanks to you I am now not that person. It's only this that can explain my sheer audacity to ignore how bizarre my question is. I've rehearsed a hundred times how I could phrase it and now I've stammered and fumbled it; but it's too late to take it back. Now you know! Am I not an idiot? Haven't I offended you and made an awful fool of myself?"

She said quietly to him but with plain speech, "You're no fool! You feel what you feel but you have endured many losses and you will accept my being unable to share your desire. Friendship is all I have to offer and it probably will be all I will ever have to offer. Please don't ever speak of more. I do care for you but your questions force me to say plain things that *must* bring you anguish and I truly fear they will drive you back into a darkness I can't even imagine. I would say that appearance matters none at all but that wouldn't be how I feel. I don't know where friendship becomes romantic love—they merge somewhere and I don't know where that somewhere is. But I know they differ and I know that physical attraction enters the equation. I do not love you in that way and I don't expect that I ever could."

"And you can't possibly feel romantic about me because of how I am," he sighed. "I *do* understand and I knew it couldn't be otherwise but the miracle of our beautiful friendship made me a fool and foolishness took over. I will *not* speak of it again. What I have with you is precious enough and it's wrong of me to ask for what you clearly can't give—how could you? So please, feel no guilt and know that I can live happily without romance as long as I have the treasure I already have with you."

In a day or two they both were able to put the trauma of the occasion out of their minds and filled the days with the joys and pleasures they shared. Pleasing and being pleased by the other. All awkwardness disappeared though his longing for her and that deeper intimacy remained. As long as the atmosphere was dominated by the happiness that was theirs his deeper longing was well controlled but there is a limit to how much happiness there is in happiness and there came that familiarity with the lovely things of life that reminds us there is something more in the human heart—a hunger that can never quite be satisfied.

CHAPTER 17

SETTING BEATRICE FREE

Time now wandered by, he lived with the deep ache of wanting someone understandably beyond his reach, cursing himself for his ever hoping for what he knew in his bones was impossible but the two drank as deeply as they could from the friendship.

She played and sang and he listened admiringly. Beatrice's sadness toward him and her inability to give him her heart added some sadness to her own experience and also to something she herself was beginning to feel—she missed her family.

This wasn't hidden from her close friend and the creature with the blood-red eyes, the strange misshapen body and yellowish teeth knew Beatrice was aching to see her family. Sometimes she chose to walk in the garden by herself and seemed to have lost some her interest in the marvelous library and the music room; even the stunning roses got less attention. She went to bed earlier she ate less, she sang and played less and when she did it was mainly sad music and sad songs. Her sadness affected his happiness and he too began to feel not only a bit unhappy but not as well as he had felt. His energy was draining away; his features were losing some of that almost spirited look it had gained. Then in the music room late one evening he heard her sing a song of home.

It was afternoon, the rain was tapping on the window and they sat in the comfortable sitting room before a lovely fire of dancing flames and talkative firewood. Phillip broke a long silence. "You're sad and I know you long for home, my dear, Beatrice. I've watched it long enough and I must let you go back to your family. There's only misery for me while you are sad and lonely. Better than one of us suffer than both. I can't pretend that your leaving won't hurt me beyond words but to keep you here would bring me no joy and you would be nothing but my prisoner. I have been crassly selfish most of my life but I finally found in you a friend who has transformed me..."

(She tearfully interrupts him) "I'm sorry I'm making you sad. I truly am and I've tried to hide it. Aside from my family I have never had a friend as warm and patient as you."

(He interrupts her) "Hush, my love, I know you've been wrestling with the loneliness and I know too that you love me. But it is what it is. We mustn't both endure this; you must go home. You've given me a renewed strength and years of lovely occasions and experiences I can feed on and be sustained by. I can and do and will cherish the light that's broken through the gloom because you are in this world and I will think of your happiness at home and that will at times fill me with happiness so great that I'll be able to hold darkness at bay. Perhaps, I'm not sure, but perhaps the lasting things you've done for me is to make me believe that there are beautiful people in the world for whom ugliness and difference do not have the final word."

(She again) "I've no wish to leave you here alone this way for always for now I know that your unending loneliness would only be my constant heartache. We must and will be the dearest friends until our lives are done. Maybe if you would allow me to visit them for a month I give you my word that I would return…"

(he interrupts) "No, my dear Beatrice, no, you must go free. No more conditions. I was wrong to force your father into such an agreement. It was a monstrous thing created by a monster and I no longer want to be that monster, nor will I be. I know you cannot love me as I would wish and you know I cannot not love you and long for you to be more than my dearest friend but to keep you here when your heart is somewhere else is not loving you. Go home, my dear, with all my heart's affection. You have given me my life back and for that I thank you. Get ready and tomorrow I will take you to the edge of the forest and someone will see you safely home."

The strongest light in this lovely room was the light from the fire that flickered on both their faces; Beatrice tear-filled eyes caught the light and sparkled and as she looked across at him he was gazing into the fire. The sight startled her for all of a sudden, it must have been the light, it must have been the angle of his gaze or the ways the tears in her eyes refracted the light—surely it was one of these or all of them—what she saw was not the face of her now beloved beast-friend, but a younger selfless man with a glorious aura.

"Phillip!" she gasped, and as he turned, startled by her sharp tone, she saw the face of a beast. "Nothing, my dear," she said and sunk back into the comfortable chair and wondered.

CHAPTER 18

THE RETURN TO HOME

A less grand coach waited for her as her companion walked with her toward the gate of the great fence, "Down that path you will soon see the coach that will carry you back to where you belong, my lovely Beatrice. Thank you again for these years of joy and transformation. Try not to forget me and forgive me whatever it is that you know needs forgiven." She wept and murmured something about her gratitude and then burst into sobbing. Before she knew it she had thrown her arms around his waist, nestled her head on his chest, listening to the thumping of his heart and his difficult breathing. Her act took his breath away and he, uncertain, but only for a moment, gently wrapped those strange arms around her and fell even more deeply in love with her. Then just as swiftly as she had embraced him she broke it off and ran down the path that would finally lead to the coach, to home and her ecstatic family.

CHAPTER 19

HOME, THE JOY & THE LONGING

When she arrived in the little town she had difficulty at first in finding the Pearson's home. They had moved, of course, to a grander home and all the Pearsons lived on one piece of land each family with a house suited to the needs of Beatrice's siblings and their children. Her father had a house that was also his office and was happily swamped in business and doing good.

There is no describing the laughing and crying, the shouting and clapping, the hugging and kissing, the thanking God, the showing off of grandchildren and the mesmerized looks at the maturing Beatrice, the meals of celebration, her bedroom door opened by her sisters to see if she was really asleep or if she could talk some more and tell of her adventure.

But after some weeks things settled back to a lovely predictability and life for the various families replaced the ecstasy of the early days of her return. Long conversations with her beloved father were rapturous, visits around town and to other places had the element of novelty, thoroughly enjoyable. Sights and sounds she had forgotten to remember were new—simple and pleasure-bring in their lost but found-again way. Visits to several larger cities, boat trips dressing up and going to grand affairs in a fine carriage, being there at a wonderful ballet performance or a grand opera, evenings out on occasions at the best restaurants or playing games when it suited her with village children; sitting for hours in the library where she worked some years ago and remembering. All these and more made a year fly away as quickly as ripping dates off a calendar on a wall.

CHAPTER 20

BACK TO A BELOVED FRIEND

But with increasing frequency there were nights when a great loneliness crept into her bedroom and wouldn't leave until she acknowledged its real presence and embraced it as her own. She thought of him, Phillip, her beast-friend who, for her if for no other, was no longer a beast but her friend. She thought of the pleasant company she had been enjoying for these many months that contrasted so starkly with his isolation. She thought of the transformation of the Pearson family's fortunes, her father's rescue and how he had been enabled to do so many gracious things for other strugglers. She thought of how much they owed comfort and joy to him — how much *she* owed to him, her heart filled again and again with unutterable gratitude but it was more than gratitude she felt. She wept again and again in the night, pitying him in his awful loneliness but it was more than pity she felt. She missed him, missed being with him, talking, walking, listening to and watching the world with him. There were times when she thought what she felt included romantic love for him but once she focused on his awful appearance she consciously focused on the depth and pleasure of friendship, just friendship. She wished she could see him or at least contact him and write to him but she didn't know how and finally wasn't even sure if she really wanted to. People in emotional phases do, say and think things they later think were silly.

But she didn't have to work it all out for one day a man, a complete stranger to the region, came to the door—a man who would answer no questions, a man who wouldn't speak a word other than that he had a letter for Miss Beatrice Pearson; a man who spoke no word to anyone in or around the town. He gave it to her and left without a word. She recognized the scrawl and knew immediately she would want to respond to the letter so she ran out of the house, looked for the man and saw him leaving their property. As fast as she could she ran after him, caught up with him before he drove off and asked him if he could get a letter to the one who gave him this one. He said he could and said he was well-paid to deliver the one she had in her hand. She got the meaning and said, "I will pay you well. Do what you must to return my letter to him." She brought him back to the house and had him wait while she hurriedly responded. She said very little but she said this: *"Send for me. Let me come to you. Your forever friend, B."* He took the letter and the generous pay and off he went. She asked no question about how the note would finally reach him but prayed that it would indeed get there.

That evening she sat with her father and told him she was going back to see the mysterious lord of the manor. She didn't know how long she would be gone but she reminded him of what he already knew—no harm would befall her there. She was free to return any time she wished and for any reason, she said. She asked him to keep her purpose to himself and to tell the family of it only when she had left. She reminded him too of what he already knew that nothing was to be said to anyone about the benefactor's whereabouts. Henry felt the sadness such a parent would feel yet he was happy that his beautiful daughter knew what she was doing in returning to her friend.

She went to her room and read again for maybe the tenth time the brief note. *"My love, I just want you to know that I have not regretted for a moment urging you to return to your home and I think of the joy that you must be feeling to be there with your beloved ones. That vision makes me smile though it doesn't look much like a smile. I expect you would be thinking of me now and then and I want you to know that I'm still living well on the wonder and beauty of our time together. Friends always, P"*

A week passed and then another and Beatrice knew the letter had never reached him. She wept sometimes and felt guilty about something she was not guilty of. She walked alone and fretted and wept some more until one mid-morning with steady rain falling she walked down the past to the gate and saw a man leaning on it. "Miss Beatrice?" he asked. She nodded. "I have a carriage to take you to a place." Wide-eyed, she said, "Let me go and get some things" and began to run back up the path. "You need absolutely nothing Miss Beatrice," he shouted after her, "I have everything!" She stopped, turned and then said, "Wait!" She ran into the house, grabbed a pen and wrote in very large letters. *"GONE! mio padre. Love, B"* and placed it in his favorite chair. Then she ran down the path toward the driver who moved toward a truly grand carriage, opened the door, offered help she didn't need and she virtually threw herself into the luxurious that would be her home for a few days.

They arrived safe and sound at the gate of the great fence where the coachman said goodbye and she, her heart beating faster than she knew it could ran to the house, pushed the big familiar door and shouted "Phillip!" There was no answer. She shouted again and again but no answer. She looked in a few rooms, he wasn't there, and she raced upstairs toward his room. "Don't you be jumping out on me!" she shouted laughing. More silence and she knocked on the door. Then she heard the words, "My Beatrice, my beloved Beatrice." She opened the door and there on a large chair he sat. Still the beast-man but now looking older, feebler and breathing with even more difficulty.

"Ah, my love," he said not much beyond a whisper. "how good of you to come." Shocked, she moved closer. This wasn't the energetic, vital person that had been capable of violent rage and great exuberance only a year ago. "I couldn't wait to get here," she said stunned. "I missed you terribly." Closer still she came. "Tell me what is wrong with you. You must be ill. Why did you not tell me? I would have come sooner. You must surely have known that. Why didn't you send for me?"

"You were where you belonged my love."

"I belong with you when you are ill."

"You belong where some young man could love you…"

"I belong with my dearest friend," she said, interrupting him.

She closed the remaining gap between them and got to her knees and put her face on his knee. He reached and rested his hand on her head and stroked her hair and whispered how he had missed her and how he was so glad that he could see her for the last time.

Sharply, she raised her head and just as sharply said, "What do you mean, 'for the last time'?"

"I am feeling very ill and weary beyond words," he said, "and I know I will be leaving before long."

"You will not die," she said. "You must not die—not now that I've found you again. I have not come to visit. I have come to stay with you until my life is done. You have entered my life and whatever we have together we will have it for the rest of our lives—but not now, not so soon."

"You are not going back home after a while?" he wheezed.

"I am not! This is now my home unless you do not want me here."

"Not want you here? I would never want you anywhere else if this is where you'd want to be. For you, if I could do it, I'd buy heaven. To bring you joy and happiness is every breath I take; it's every beat of my heart. The only joy left me now is *your* joy. Though I never would have told you, it was losing your presence that drained from me my desire to live and since then I have grown weaker and weaker. I think you have come in time to say goodbye to one who loves you more than life."

She looked long at him in silence and then said, "I have come in time to claim my husband so he better not die."

He began to make mournful sounds and shake. "Please, you must not say such things when you know they cannot happen. I need you to comfort me with words of truth—truth I need now, not impossible dreams."

"Of this I'm sure," she said, "they will be impossible dreams if you refuse to live, if you insist on dying and breaking my heart. If I cannot marry you I will marry no one else. They spoke for another while and since both were weary they agreed to sleep. In the morning she made her way to Lino and Mariana and learned that the lord of the manor hadn't touched food in nearly a week. They discussed the matter and the couple advised this and that to meet the situation and so it began. Beatrice would bring food to his room and eat with him there and within another week she saw a marked improvement. The food was doing what food is supposed to do but the presence of his beloved friend was perhaps doing even more.

CHAPTER 21

THE MIRACULOUS POWER OF LOVE

His energy level increased, his voice grew stronger, his responses quickened, he slept more soundly and the wheezing that had always been present but had worsened began to diminish—his breathing was returning in strength and depth. In a month he was more like his energetic self. Short walks, good food, fresh air and the company of one who filled up his senses was winning the war.

Another something like three months he was fully back to health with which he could take the full pleasure of the joys of life though it's true there were some obvious limitations. But there was more than a renewed appreciation of the pleasures there was a freshness about him—about himself! It was a freshness not discernible the way one sees a stone or a tree; it was more sensed than seen and as weeks passed the aged look that had been there due to the illness was gone and a new glow took its place. The laughter was back, the music and song, the praise of the roses, the reading came back and she read sections to him in the evening as they sat by that wondrous fireplace with the dancing flames in it and an occasional muttered protest from Schubert who wanted silence.

She finished the reading one evening and the light was purposely dimmed so they could better enjoy the big lovely fire. It happened again! Once before she went away she glanced from the flames to his face as he looked in the flames and she saw a younger man. She had been riveted and then called his name but when he turned to look there were the same bestial features.

It did—it happened again, and again she was startled. "Phillip," she said, and he turned to look at her and though he wasn't a young man by any means there was a change! She rose, increased the light and looked carefully without showing that she was doing it. The change didn't seem as marked as it did in the dimmer light. What was she thinking, she asked herself but it is a bit of magic how a different angle in a different light-setting reveals things not seen in customary situations.

She lowered the light again and turned on some pleasant music. "Beautiful," he said. "Have you ever danced, my love?" She told him she never had. Would you like to learn some day, he wanted to know and she thought, yes, maybe she would. "Let's start now," he said, rising and reaching for her hand. She was reluctant but she took it and he drew her close, gave some simple instructions and they moved together some. It wasn't bad for a beginner and he made her believe she was a natural. It pleased her but something else took her attention—it was his hands. She shifted her own so she could explore his without showing that's what she was doing. Her heart skipped, his fingers were definitely less gnarled, straighter and unless, she told herself, unless she was imagining it, there was a little less hair on his hands. Afraid to express herself on it and yet too excited not to she said, working to make it sound casual, "You know sometimes I imagine that your hands are improving their shape."

His response excited her even more. "I didn't want to say anything about it in case it was wishful thinking but I thought the same thing a day or two ago." That was the end of the dancing lesson and the light was increased and together they examined his hands. There was no doubt about it, the shape and size of his fingers *had* changed a little and some of the hair had disappeared. They looked at each other with hope written all over their faces. Being completely healed of an illness is what we do and should look for—there's no getting away from that but there's something about the beginning and the experience of getting better and better that has a glory and a joy all its own. The completed cure closes the book happily but convalescence, a lengthy awareness of the turn of the tide against the enemy prolongs the pleasure.

Together they watched with mounting excitement the slow but discernible progress. How far will it go? All the way to complete cure? That hope made the complete cure present in their minds so that they were exulting in it long before it came if indeed it arrived. The drum roll before the trapeze artist lets go of her bar to complete a triple somersault high above the ground! The operatic overture that announces the rising of the great curtain before the opera actually begins! Every tiny but real reduction in the swelling of a jaw, every tiny change in the redness of an eye, and ear not quite as tortured as it was last month or teeth not just a tiny bit whiter than they had been—these and more changes were promises and they heralded a new day and a new world was coming.

Phillip was beside himself with excitement but it would be difficult to say who was most thrilled or smiled the widest or applauded the hardest for every little victory against a vicious enemy—Phillip or the young woman who loved her friend Phillip more than Phillip did. Other than, now and then, fearful moments triggered by a reappearance of something life was all joy, all hope and dancing.

On that eventful evening the soft music played as they held one another and she, tired but not willing to end it yet, laid her head against his chest, wondrously happy. "Phillip," he heard her say in a getting-sleepy voice, "I love you." He held her closer and loved the moment. "I know you do, my dear and it's wonderful."

Still close she leaned her head back and looked up at him. "No you don't. I'm in love with you, my dear. It's more than friendship now, Phillip." He wanted to talk all night and tell her how incredible, inexpressible, unfathomable, immeasurable, indescribable and other things the news was that she had fallen in love with him. But she was weary and finally she slumped back in the chair fast asleep. He lifted her gently and carried her to her room, laid her on the bed, covered her with a blanket and noted before he turned out the light that she smiled in her sleep.

Breakfast was eaten late but Jennifer and Lino's delicious food was kept warm in the specially made dishes. When Phillip came to the table the first thing Beatrice noticed were his eyes—they were no longer a deep red but a salmon pink. The difference was remarkable! He saw her looking in happy surprise and smiled and his teeth were whiter and nearer back to where they belonged and his gums had shrunk considerably. The speed with which he was healing and changing was a marvel.

"How can this be happening," she whispered in awe. He reached and took her hand in his, which had begun to look like a healthy human hand. "It's happening because I am in love and I am loved by the most beautiful woman I have ever met. When you returned many months ago I was dying and you loved me back to life not by a witch's wand or mystic spells but just by being you toward me. That love released power in me that I had no desire to put to use — why would I want it when all I loved and wanted to live for was far away? Who in this world would have thought that you, dearest Beatrice, would have befriended one such as I have been? And then, perhaps even more mysterious and wonderful, friendship became romance. If I am being transformed, and I am, it is only because your love inspired the power of my immune system to defeat the curse I feel I brought on myself. You made we *want* to live and to be near you always, loving you and being loved by you. Two friends who found another love along the way; a love that is enriched and safe-guarded not by physical beauty or possessions but by a deeper love that seeks not its own but the joy and blessing of the other.

Beatrice wept with pleasure at the tone and the words and even more, at the heart the words and tone came from. "I beg you," he said, "don't grow weary of my telling you what you have done for me. My words are for you but they're as much for me as you for I cannot keep them in. It is beauty that saved the beast."

She raised her head, the tears falling, "Beast? What Beast? I know no Beast nor have I ever known one."

In a few more months he was the handsome man he had once been. Now no longer a prisoner the gate was thrown open. The Pearsons and all their friends and neighbors were carried to the grand affair in a line of grand carriages and witnessed their marriage.

Made in the USA
Lexington, KY
26 February 2018